The BOOK of GIVING

The BOOK of

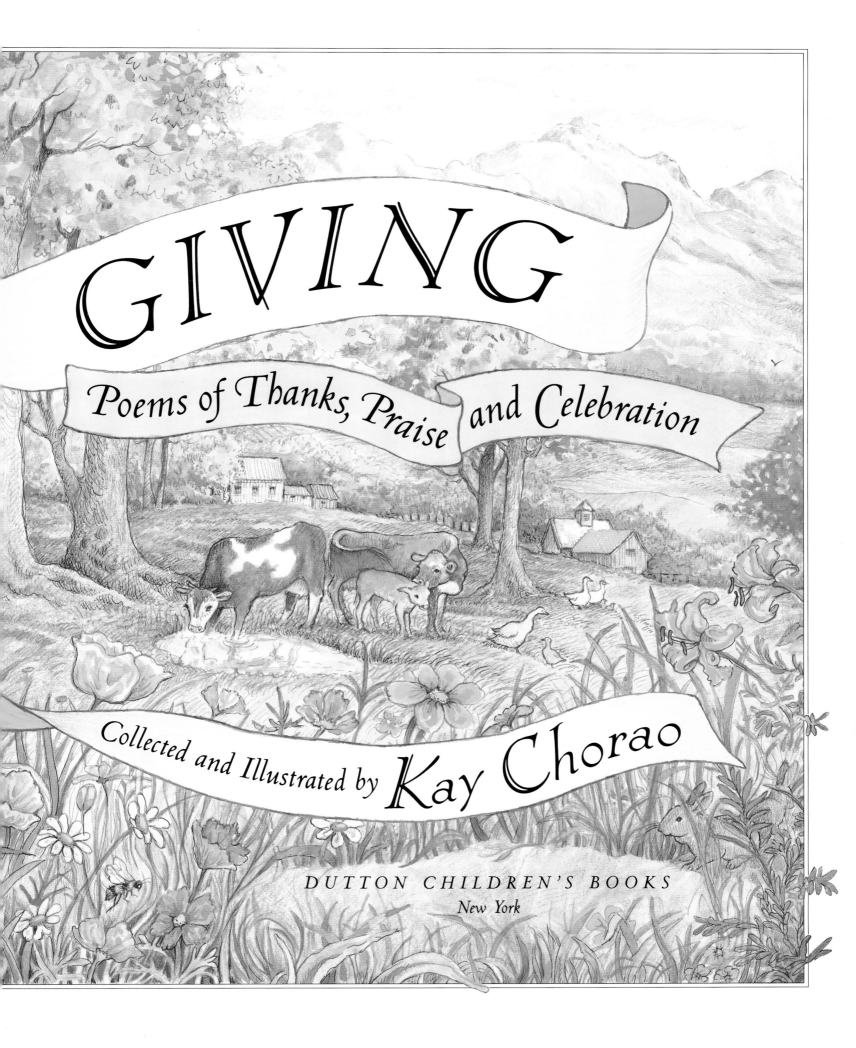

GIVING

Poems of Thanks, Praise and Celebration

Collected and Illustrated by *Kay Chorao*

DUTTON CHILDREN'S BOOKS
New York

Library of Congress Cataloging-in-Publication Data

The book of giving: poems of thanks, praise, and celebration/
collected and illustrated by Kay Chorao.
p. cm.
Includes index.
Summary: A collection of poems celebrating the act
of giving and the joy of receiving.
ISBN 0-525-45409-8 (hardcover)
1. Generosity—Juvenile poetry. 2. Children's poetry, American.
3. Children's poetry, English. 4. Gratitude—Juvenile poetry.
5. Praise—Juvenile poetry.
[1. Generosity—Poetry. 2. Gratitude—Poetry.
3. Poetry—Collections.]
I. Chorao, Kay.
PS595.G38B66 1995
808.81'9353—dc20 95-12796
CIP AC

Published in the United States in 1995 by
Dutton Children's Books,
a division of Penguin Books USA Inc.
375 Hudson Street, New York, New York 10014
Designed by Sara Reynolds
Printed in Italy
First Edition
1 3 5 7 9 10 8 6 4 2

To Jamie, Peter, and Ian

K. C.

CONTENTS

ACKNOWLEDGMENTS

Every effort has been made to trace the copyright holders of the material included in this anthology. The publisher regrets any possible omissions and would be glad to hear from any current copyright holder whose name does not appear below.

"Up from the bed of the river" (originally entitled "The Creation"), from *God's Trombones* by James Weldon Johnson. Copyright © 1927 The Viking Press, Inc., copyright renewed © 1955 by Grace Nail Johnson. Used by permission of Viking Penguin, a division of Penguin Books USA Inc. "Rock, Rock, Sleep, My Baby," from *Father Fox's Pennyrhymes* by Clyde Watson. Text copyright © 1971 by Clyde Watson. Selection reprinted by permission of HarperCollins Publishers. Reprinted in the United Kingdom by permission of Curtis Brown Ltd. Copyright © 1971 by Clyde Watson. First appeared in *Father Fox's Pennyrhymes*, published by T. Y. Crowell. "Little," from *Everything and Anything* by Dorothy Aldis. Reprinted by permission of G. P. Putnam's Sons. Copyright © 1925-1927, copyright renewed © 1953-1955 by Dorothy Aldis. "Morning Has Broken," by Eleanor Farjeon. Reprinted by permission of Harold Ober Associates. Copyright © 1957 by Eleanor Farjeon. "Father," from *The Malibu and Other Poems* by Myra Cohn Livingston. Copyright © 1972 by Myra Cohn Livingston. Reprinted by permission of Marian Reiner. "Daddy," by Rose Fyleman. Reprinted by permission of The Society of Authors as the literary representative of the Estate of Rose Fyleman. Published in the United States by Bantam Doubleday Dell Publishing Group, Inc. "You be saucer," from *You Be Good & I'll Be Night* by Eve Merriam (Morrow Junior Books). Copyright © 1988 by Eve Merriam. Reprinted by permission of Marian Reiner. "Granny Granny Please Comb My Hair," by Grace Nichols. Reprinted by permission of Curtis Brown Ltd, London, on behalf of Grace Nichols. Copyright © 1984 Grace Nichols. "Mother to Son" and "Piggy-Back," from *Selected Poems* by Langston Hughes. Copyright © 1926 by Alfred A. Knopf, Inc. and copyright renewed © 1954 by Langston Hughes. Reprinted by permission of the publisher. Reprinted in the United Kingdom by permission of Harold Ober Associates. "Dunce Song 6," from *Collected and New Poems 1924-1963* by Mark Van Doren. Copyright © 1963 by Mark Van Doren and copyright renewed © 1991 by Dorothy G. Van Doren. Reprinted by permission of Hill and Wang, a division of Farrar, Straus & Giroux, Inc. "Childhood Painting Lesson," by Henry Rago. Copyright © 1953, 1981 by Henry Rago. Originally printed in *The New Yorker*. Reprinted by permission. "Direction," by Alonzo Lopez, from *Whispering Wind* by Terry Allen. Copyright © 1972 by the Institute of American Indian Arts. Used by permission of Doubleday, a division of Bantam Doubleday Dell Publishing Group, Inc. "For a Bird," from *The Moon and a Star* by Myra Cohn Livingston. Copyright © 1965, 1993 by Myra Cohn Livingston. Reprinted by permission of Marian Reiner. "To a Squirrel at Kyle-na-no," from *The Poems of W. B. Yeats: A New Edition*, edited by Richard J. Finneran (New York: Macmillan, 1983). Reprinted by permission of Simon & Schuster, Inc. "A Mother," by Issa, from *Year of My Life: A Translation of Issa's "Oraga Haru"* by Nobuyuki Yuasa. Copyright © 1972. Reprinted by permission of the University of California Press. "The Herd-Boy's Song" and "The Moon in the Mountains," by Chen Shan-min, from *The Dragon Book*, translated by E. D. Edwards, published by William Hodge and Company, Ltd. Reprinted by permission of David Higham Associates, Ltd. "Dear Father," from *A Child's Good Night Book* by Margaret Wise Brown. Copyright © 1943 by Margaret Wise Brown. Reprinted by permission of HarperCollins Publishers. "A little yellow cricket" (originally entitled "Cricket"), from *Singing for Power: The Song Magic of the Papago Indians of Southern Arizona* by Ruth Murray Underhill. Copyright © 1938, 1966 by Ruth Murray Underhill. "Sing a Song of Juniper," from *Robert Francis: Collected Poems, 1936-1976* (Amherst: University of Massachusetts Press, 1976). Copyright © 1976 by Robert Francis. "Thanksgiving," from *Cherry Stones! Garden Swings!* by Ivy O. Eastwick. Copyright renewed © 1990 by Hooper & Wollen. Reprinted by permission of Abingdon Press. "Light Another Candle," by Miriam Chaikin, from *A New Treasury of Children's Poetry* (New York: Doubleday, 1984). Poem copyright © 1984 by Miriam Chaikin. Reprinted by permission of McIntosh and Otis, Inc. "The Christmas Present," from *The Apple Vendor's Fair* by Patricia Hubbell. Copyright © 1963 and copyright renewed © 1991 by Patricia Hubbell. Reprinted by permission of Atheneum Books for Young Readers, an imprint of Simon & Schuster Children's Publishing Division. "Surprises," by Jean Conder Soule. Reprinted by permission of the author, who holds all rights. "Secrets," by Elsie Melchert Fowler, from *Jack and Jill*, copyright © 1939 by The Curtis Publishing Company. Reprinted by permission of Children's Better Health Institute, Benjamin Franklin Literary & Medical Society, Inc., Indianapolis, IN. "Dandelions," from *Around and About* by Marchette Chute, copyright © 1957 by E. P. Dutton, copyright renewed © 1984 by Marchette Chute. Reprinted by permission of Elizabeth Roach. "Dreams," from *The Dream Keeper and Other Poems* by Langston Hughes. Copyright © 1932 by Alfred A. Knopf, Inc. and copyright renewed © 1960 by Langston Hughes. Reprinted by permission of the publisher. "A Riddle," from *All That Sunlight* by Charlotte Zolotow. Copyright © 1967 by Charlotte Zolotow. Reprinted by permission of the author. "Mr. Minnitt," by Rose Fyleman. Reprinted by permission of The Society of Authors as the literary representative of the Estate of Rose Fyleman. "Joe," from *Far and Few* by David McCord. Copyright © 1952 by David McCord. Reprinted by permission of Little, Brown and Company. "Homage to God," from the *UNICEF Book of Children's Poems.* Copyright © 1970 by William I. Kaufman. Reprinted by permission of the author.

INTRODUCTION

This collection was created in hopes of encouraging children to think about giving—in all its facets. In addition to the familiar and eagerly anticipated giving of holiday and birthday presents, there is the giving of time, care, advice, joy, thanks, and, above all, love. And these occur among all age groups and in every culture. Think of a parent cradling her child, a little girl saving an injured bird, or a grandfather offering the wisdom of his years. Sharing this book should help children appreciate and give their own thanks for special people, things, and times, many of which are universal.

Consider, too, the generous gifts of the natural world: beauty, protection, abundance, and resources from trees, plants, flowers, and the animals that share our fragile planet. And finally, consider the mysterious, miraculous gift of life itself.

This collection starts with two poems praising God's creation and ends with a prayer of thanks to Him. In between are poems that range from playful to serious and are meant to suggest the many joyful ways that giving is woven through our lives and the wonderful world that sustains us.

Up from the bed of the river

Up from the bed of the river
God scooped the clay;
And by the bank of the river
He kneeled him down;
And there the great God Almighty
Who lit the sun and fixed it in the sky
Who flung the stars to the most far corner of the night,
Who rounded the earth in the middle of his hand;
This Great God,
Like a mammy bending over her baby,
Kneeled down in the dust
Toiling over a lump of clay
Till he shaped it in his own image;

Then into it he blew the breath of life,
And man became a living soul.
Amen. Amen.

James Weldon Johnson
From *The Creation*

Dakota Prairie Hymn

Many and great, O God, are Thy things
Maker of Earth and Sky.
Thy hands have set
The heavens with stars
Thy fingers spread
The mountains and plains.
Lo, at Thy word
The waters were formed
Deep seas obey Thy voice.

Native American prayer

Six Weeks Old

He is so small, he does not know
The summer sun, the winter snow;
The spring that ebbs and comes again,
All this is far beyond his ken.

A little world he feels and sees:
His mother's arms, his mother's knees;
He hides his face against her breast,
And does not care to learn the rest.

Christopher Morley

Rock, Rock, Sleep, My Baby

Rock, rock, sleep, my baby
Sings the sweet cuckoo…
When your Daddy comes back home
He'll bring a toy for you.

Hush, hush, sleep, my baby
Sleep the whole night through…
When your Daddy comes back home
He'll sing a song for you.

Clyde Watson

Little

I am the sister of him
And he is my brother.
He is too little for us
To talk to each other.

So every morning I show him
My doll and my book;
But every morning he still is
Too little to look.

Dorothy Aldis

Morning Has Broken

Morning has broken
Like the first morning,
Blackbird has spoken
Like the first bird.
Praise for the singing!
Praise for the morning!
Praise for them, springing
Fresh from the Word!

Sweet the rain's new fall
Sunlit from heaven,
Like the first dewfall
On the first grass.
Praise for the sweetness
Of the wet garden,
Sprung in completeness
Where his feet pass.

Mine is the sunlight!
Mine is the morning
Born of the one light
Eden saw play!
Praise with elation,
Praise every morning,
God's re-creation
Of the new day!

Eleanor Farjeon

May the road rise to meet you

May the road rise to meet you,
May the wind be always at your back,
May the sun shine warm on your face,
The rain fall softly on your fields,
And until we meet again
May God hold you in the palm of his hand.

Traditional Irish folk blessing

For, lo, the winter is past

For, lo, the winter is past,
The rain is over and gone;
The flowers appear on the earth;
The time of the singing of birds is come,
And the voice of the turtle is heard in our land.

The Bible
Song of Solomon 2:11–12

Father

Carrying my world
Your head tops ceilings.
Your shoulders split door frames.
Your back holds up walls.

You are bigger than all sounds of laughter,
                                    of weeping,
Your hand in mine keeps us straight ahead.

Myra Cohn Livingston

Daddy

When Daddy shaves and lets me stand and look,
I like it better than a picture-book.
He pulls such lovely faces all the time
Like funny people in a pantomime.

Rose Fyleman

You be saucer

You be saucer,
I'll be cup,
piggyback, piggyback,
pick me up.

You be tree,
I'll be pears,
carry me, carry me
up the stairs.

You be Good,
I'll be Night,
tuck me in, tuck me in
nice and tight.

Eve Merriam

Granny Granny
Please Comb My Hair

Granny Granny
please comb my hair
you always take your time
you always take such care

You put me to sit on a cushion
between your knees
you rub a little coconut oil
parting gentle as a breeze

Mummy Mummy
she's always in a hurry-hurry
rush
she pulls my hair
sometimes she tugs

But Granny
you have all the time in the world
and when you're finished
you always turn my head and say
"Now who's a nice girl."

Grace Nichols

Mother to Son

Well, son, I'll tell you:
Life for me ain't been no crystal stair.
It's had tacks in it,
And splinters,
And boards torn up,
And places with no carpet on the floor—
Bare.
But all the time
I'se been a-climbin' on,
And reachin' landin's,
And turnin' corners,
And sometimes goin' in the dark

Where there ain't been no light.
So, boy, don't you turn back.
Don't you set down on the steps
'Cause you finds it kinder hard.
Don't you fall now—
For I'se still goin', honey,
I'se still climbin',
And life for me ain't been no crystal stair.

Langston Hughes

Grandma's Lost Balance

"What is the matter, grandmother dear?
Come, let me help you. Sit down here
And rest, and I'll fan you while you tell
How it was that you almost fell."
"I slipped a bit where the walk was wet
And lost my balance, my little pet!"
"Lost your balance? Oh, never mind it,
You sit still and I'll go and find it."

Sydney Dayre (Mrs. Cochran)

Piggy-Back

My daddy rides me piggy-back.
My mama rides me, too.
But grandma says her poor old back
Has had enough to do.

Langston Hughes

Dunce Song 6

Her hand in my hand,
Soft as the south wind,
Soft as a colt's nose,
Soft as forgetting;

Her cheek to my cheek,
Red as the cranberry,
Red as a mitten,
Red as remembering—

Here we go round like raindrops,
Raindrops,
Here we go round
So snug together,

Oh, but I wonder,
Oh, but I know,
Who comforts like raisins,
Who kisses like snow.

Mark Van Doren

When I walk through thy woods

When I walk through thy woods,
may my right foot and my left foot
be harmless to the little creatures
that move in its grasses: as it is said
by the mouth of thy prophet,
They shall not hurt nor destroy
in all my holy mountain.
Amen.

Rabbi Moshe Hakotun

Childhood Painting Lesson

"Draw me," the cypress said.
"I will hold quite still and bow my head."

"Draw us," the willows cried.
"We will lift our gentle skirts aside."

The poppies called, "We will give you red."
"I will give you silver," the river said.

I recall on this neglected lawn
How the world knelt sweetly to be drawn.

Henry Rago

Direction

I was directed by my grandfather
To the East,
    so I might have the power of the bear;
To the South,
    so I might have the courage of the eagle;
To the West,
    so I might have the wisdom of the owl;
To the North,
    so I might have the craftiness of the fox;
To the Earth,
    so I might receive her fruit;
To the Sky,
    so I might lead a life of innocence.

Alonzo Lopez

A Friend in the Garden

He is not John the gardener,
    And yet the whole day long
Employs himself most usefully
    The flower-beds among.
He is not Tom the pussy-cat;
    And yet the other day,
With stealthy stride and glistening eye,
    He crept upon his prey.

He is not Dash, the dear old dog,
    And yet, perhaps, if you
Took pains with him and petted him,
    You'd come to love him, too.
He's not a blackbird, though he chirps,
    And though he once was black;
But now he wears a loose, grey coat,
    All wrinkled on the back.

He's got a very dirty face,
    And very shining eyes!
He sometimes comes and sits indoors;
    He looks—and p'r'aps is—wise.
But in a sunny flower-bed
    He has his fixed abode;
He eats the things that eat my plants—
    He is a friendly TOAD.

Juliana Horatia Ewing

Hurt No Living Thing

Hurt no living thing;
Ladybird, nor butterfly,
Nor moth with dusty wing,
Nor cricket chirping cheerily,
Nor grasshopper so light of leap,
Nor dancing gnat, nor beetle fat,
Nor harmless worms that creep.

Christina Rossetti

For a Bird

I found him lying near the tree;
    I folded up his wings.
Oh, little bird,
You never heard
The song the summer sings.

I wrapped him in a shirt I wore in winter;
    it was blue.
Oh, little bird,
You never heard
The song I sang to you.

Myra Cohn Livingston

Feather or Fur

When you watch for
Feather or fur
Feather or fur
Do not stir
Do not stir.

Feather or fur
Come crawling
Creeping
Some come peeping
Some by night
And some by day.
Most come gently
All come softly
Do not scare
A friend away.

When you watch for
Feather or fur
Feather or fur
Do not stir
Do not stir.

John Becker

To a Squirrel
at Kyle-na-no

Come play with me;
Why should you run
Through the shaking tree
As though I'd a gun
To strike you dead?
When all I would do
Is to scratch your head
And let you go.

William Butler Yeats

A Mother

A mother horse
Keeps watch
While her child
Drinks.

Issa

The Sheep

"Lazy sheep, pray tell me why
In the pleasant fields you lie,
Eating grass, and daisies white,
From the morning till the night?
Every thing can something do,
But what kind of use are you?"

"Nay, my little master, nay,
Do not serve me so, I pray;
Don't you see the wool that grows
On my back, to make you clothes?
Cold, and very cold, you'd be
If you had not wool from me.

"True, it seems a pleasant thing,
To nip the daisies in the spring;
But many chilly nights I pass
On the cold and dewy grass,
Or pick a scanty dinner, where
All the common's brown and bare.

"Then the farmer comes at last,
When the merry spring is past,
And cuts my woolly coat away,
To warm you in the winter's day:
Little master, this is why
In the pleasant fields I lie."

Ann and Jane Taylor

Out in the Fields

The little cares that fretted me,
    I lost them yesterday
Among the fields above the sea,
    Among the winds that play,
Among the lowing of the herds,
    The rustling of the trees,
Among the singing of the birds,
    The humming of the bees.

The foolish fears of what might pass
    I cast them all away
Among the clover-scented grass,
    Among the new-mown hay,
Among the hushing of the corn,
    Where drowsy poppies nod,
Where ill thoughts die and good are born—
    Out in the fields of God.

Anonymous

The Herd-Boy's Song

Splashing water,
Luscious grass;
Somebody's child is herding an ox,
Riding his ox by the river-side.
Browsing ox,
Happy youth;
Somebody's child is singing a song,
Shouting his song to a little white cloud:

Away at morn my ox I ride,
And back again at eventide.

My two feet never touch the dust;
In wealth and fame who puts his trust?

My rush hat shelters me from rain;
In silk and sables what's to gain?

I quench my thirst at a mountain rill;
Who'd spend a fortune his belly to fill?

When the sun on his golden horse rides high
Down by the river go ox and I;

When the sinking sun makes shadows creep
He carries me home on his back, asleep.

Chen Shan-min

The Moon in the Mountains

Here in the mountains the moon I love,
Hanging alight in a distant grove;
Pitying me in my loneliness,
She reaches a finger and touches my dress.
My heart resembles the moon;
The moon resembles my heart.
My heart and the moon in each other delight,
Each watching the other throughout the long night.

Chen Shan-min

Songs of Innocence: Introduction

Piping down the valleys wild,
Piping songs of pleasant glee,
On a cloud I saw a child,
And he laughing said to me:

"Pipe a song about a Lamb!"
So I piped with merry chear.
"Piper, pipe that song again";
So I piped: he wept to hear.

"Drop thy pipe, thy happy pipe;
Sing thy songs of happy chear";
So I sung the same again
While he wept with joy to hear.

"Piper, sit thee down and write
In a book, that all may read."
So he vanish'd from my sight,
And I pluck'd a hollow reed,

And I made a rural pen,
And I stain'd the water clear,
And I wrote my happy songs
Every child may joy to hear.

William Blake

I Heard a Bird Sing

I heard a bird sing
    In the dark of December
A magical thing
    And sweet to remember.

"We are nearer to Spring
    Than we were in September,"
I heard a bird sing
    In the dark of December.

Oliver Herford

Dear Father

Dear Father
hear and bless
thy beasts and
singing birds.
And guard with
tenderness
small things
that have
no words.

Margaret Wise Brown

The Cow

The friendly cow all red and white,
    I love with all my heart;
She gives me cream with all her might,
    To eat with apple tart.

She wanders lowing here and there,
    And yet she cannot stray,
All in the pleasant open air,
    The pleasant light of day;

And blown by all the winds that pass
    And wet with all the showers,
She walks among the meadow grass
    And eats the meadow flowers.

Robert Louis Stevenson

A Kitten's Thought

It's very nice to think of how
In every country lives a Cow
To furnish milk with all her might
For Kitten's comfort and delight.

Oliver Herford

A little yellow cricket

A little yellow cricket
At the roots of the corn
Is hopping about and singing.

Papago Indian verse

Sing a Song of Juniper

Sing a song of juniper
Whose song is seldom sung,
Whose needles prick the finger,
Whose berries burn the tongue.

Sing a song of juniper
With boughs shaped like a bowl
For holding sun or snowfall
High on the pasture knoll.

Sing a song of juniper
Whose green is more than green,
Is blue and bronze and violet
And colors in between.

Sing a song of juniper
That keeps close to the ground,
A song composed of silence
And very little sound.

Sing a song of juniper
That hides the hunted mouse,
And gives me outdoor shadows
To haunt my indoor house.

Robert Francis

The First Bee

In the pale sunshine, with frail wings unfurled,
Comes to the bending snowdrop the first bee.
She gives her winter honey prudently;
And faint with travel in a bitter world,
The bee makes music, tentative and low,
And spring awakes and laughs across the snow.

Mary Webb
From *The Snowdrop*

A wee little worm in a hickory-nut

A wee little worm in a hickory-nut
        Sang, happy as he could be,
"O I live in the heart of the whole round world,
        And it all belongs to me!"

James Whitcomb Riley
From *A Session with Uncle Sidney*

Thanksgiving

Thank You
  for all my hands can hold—
    apples red,
      and melons gold,
        yellow corn
          both ripe and sweet,
        peas and beans
          so good to eat!

Thank You
  for all my eyes can see—
    lovely sunlight,
    field and tree,
      white cloud-boats
        in sea-deep sky,
      soaring bird
        and butterfly.

Thank You
  for all my ears can hear—
    birds' song echoing
    far and near,
      songs of little
        stream, big sea,
      cricket, bullfrog,
        duck and bee!

Ivy O. Eastwick

Light Another Candle

Let all the family gather,
bring your friends along,
light another candle,
sing another song.

It's Hanukkah, Hanukkah,
we make the candles glow
to celebrate a victory
two thousand years ago.

When ancient Jewish heroes
known as Maccabees
battled for the right
to worship as they pleased.

Come, light another candle,
make the dreidl spin,
sing yet another song, hoi!
chirry, birry, bin.

Miriam Chaikin

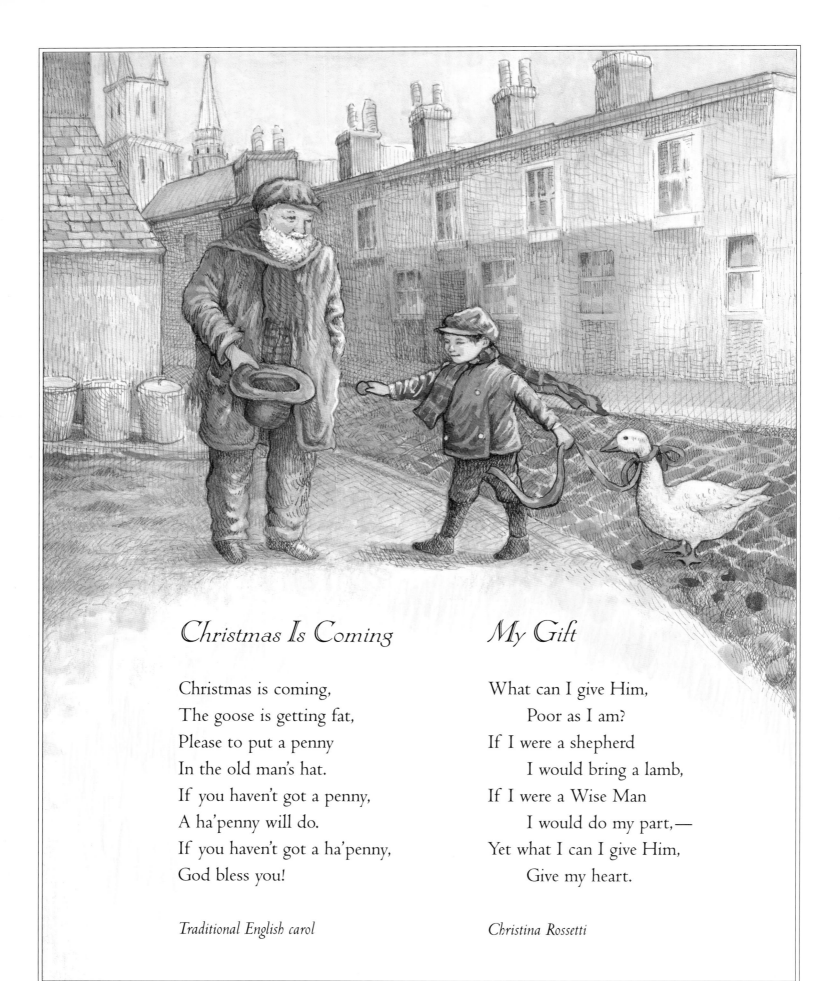

Christmas Is Coming

Christmas is coming,
The goose is getting fat,
Please to put a penny
In the old man's hat.
If you haven't got a penny,
A ha'penny will do.
If you haven't got a ha'penny,
God bless you!

Traditional English carol

My Gift

What can I give Him,
　　Poor as I am?
If I were a shepherd
　　I would bring a lamb,
If I were a Wise Man
　　I would do my part,—
Yet what I can I give Him,
　　Give my heart.

Christina Rossetti

The Friendly Beasts

Jesus, our brother, kind and good,
Was humbly born in a stable rude,
And the friendly beasts around Him stood,
Jesus, our brother, kind and good.

"I," said the donkey, shaggy and brown,
"I carried His mother uphill and down,
I carried her safely to Bethlehem town.
I," said the donkey, shaggy and brown.

"I," said the cow, all white and red,
"I gave Him my manger for His bed,
I gave Him my hay to pillow His head.
I," said the cow, all white and red.

"I," said the sheep with the curly horn,
"I gave Him my wool, for His blanket warm,
He wore my coat on Christmas morn.
I," said the sheep with the curly horn.

"I," said the dove, from the rafters high,
"Cooed Him to sleep, that He should not cry,
We cooed Him to sleep, my mate and I.
I," said the dove, from the rafters high.

So every beast, by some good spell,
In the stable dark was glad to tell
Of the gift he gave Immanuel,
The gift he gave Immanuel.

Anonymous

My Valentine

I will make you brooches and toys for your delight
Of bird-song at morning and star-shine at night.
I will make a palace fit for you and me
      Of green days in forests and blue days at sea.

Robert Louis Stevenson

People Buy a Lot of Things

People buy a lot of things—
Carts and balls and nails and rings,
But I would buy a bird that sings.

I would buy a bird that sings and let it sing for me,
And let it sing of flying things and mating in a tree,
And then I'd open wide the cage, and set the singer free.

Annette Wynne

The Christmas Present

The fields are wrapped in silver snow,
Tied tight with grey stone walls,
While cardinals flutter in the drifts
Like cheery Christmas balls.
    I wonder what the spring will shout
    When she unwraps the box
    And finds to her extreme delight
    A toad, a mole, a fox?

Patricia Hubbell

Surprises

Surprises are round
    Or long and tallish.
Surprises are square
    Or flat and smallish.

Surprises are wrapped
    With paper and bow,
And hidden in closets
    Where secrets won't show.

Surprises are often
    Good things to eat;
A get-well toy or
    A birthday treat.

Surprises come
    In such interesting sizes—
I LIKE
    SURPRISES!

Jean Conder Soule

Secrets

If you see a package
Gaily wrapped and tied,
Don't ask too many questions,
'Cause a secret is inside.

Elsie Melchert Fowler

Dandelions

I'm picking my mother a present.
    How perfectly glad she will be
To see all the beautiful flowers
    She gets on her birthday from me.

Marchette Chute

For a Birthday

So much that I would give you hovers out
Of reach of my poor giving—song within
Your heart forever, faith to end all doubt,
And laughter, warm and gold, when you begin
To grow too serious, and, always near,
The good companionship of trees and birds;
And always, for your beauty-loving ear,
Music when you have need of it, and words
That pleasure you and rest you, softly spoken;
Unnumbered good days, peace of a starry night,
And love from dawn to dawn that's an unbroken
Deep certainty in you....I have no right
To dream of it—but never doubt I should
Give you such birthday presents, if I could.

Elaine V. Emans

To the Wayfarer

A Poem Fastened to Trees in the Portuguese Forests

Ye who pass by and would raise your hand
    against me, hearken ere you harm me.

I am the heat of your hearth on the cold
    winter nights, the friendly shade screening
    you from summer sun, and my fruits are
    refreshing draughts, quenching your thirst
    as you journey on.

I am the beam that holds your house, the
    board of your table, the bed on which you
    lie, the timber that builds your boat.

I am the handle of your hoe, the door of
    your homestead, the wood of your cradle,
    and the shell of your coffin.

I am the bread of kindness and the flower
    of beauty.
Ye who pass by, listen to my prayer: harm
    me not.

Anonymous

The Rain at Night

The good rain knows when to fall,
Coming in this spring to help the seeds,
Choosing to fall by night with a friendly wind,
Silently moistening the whole earth.
Over this silent wilderness the clouds are dark.
The only light shines from a river boat.
Tomorrow morning everything will be red and wet,
And all Chengtu will be covered with blossoming flowers.

Tu Fu

I Give My Mind a Ride

All day long I must keep my mind
    in good order.
But when the day is quiet
    and I no longer must abide
I close my eyes to give
    my mind a fanciful ride
In the carriage of my imagination
    off to the playful side.

I'll imagine I'm a gust of wind
    Giving pollen a lift to a flower bed,
Or curl the ocean wave, pushing the tides ahead.

I'll imagine I'm a pillow,
    Giving your head a soft cradle,
A safe place where to weave a dreamy fable.

I'll imagine I'm a cloud
    giving a turning, churning white in vast blue
Making different shapes and sizes for you to wander to.

But now the dog is whining for his walk,
    All this folly to him is time a-wastin';
First I'll park the carriage
    of my imagination
Then my mind will step off
    as this is the final station.
For now once again, I must keep my mind
    in good order.

Ian Chorao

Dreams

Hold fast to dreams
For if dreams die
Life is a broken-winged bird
That cannot fly.

Hold fast to dreams
For when dreams go
Life is a barren field
Frozen with snow.

Langston Hughes

A Riddle

Once when I was very scared
I met a man who knew.
"How did you know?"
I said to him.
He answered, "I am, too."

Then he said something,
for me too it was true,
"But I'm not scared now
because of you."

Charlotte Zolotow

Mr. Minnitt

Mr. Minnitt mends my soles
When I have walked them into holes.
He works in such a funny place
And has a wrinkly, twinkly face.
His hands are brown and hard and thin,
His thread goes slowly out and in.
He cannot walk without a crutch—
I like him very, very much.

Rose Fyleman

Joe

We feed the birds in winter,
And outside in the snow
We have a tray of many seeds
For many birds of many breeds
And one gray squirrel named Joe.
    But Joe comes early,
    Joe comes late,
    And all the birds
    Must stand and wait.
And waiting there for Joe to go
Is pretty cold work in the snow.

David McCord

What Do We Plant

What do we plant when we plant the tree?
We plant the ship, which will cross the sea.
We plant the mast to carry the sails;
We plant the planks to withstand the gales—
The keel, the keelson, the beam, the knee;
We plant the ship when we plant the tree.

What do we plant when we plant the tree?
We plant the houses for you and me.
We plant the rafters, the shingles, the floors,
We plant the studding, the lath, the doors,
The beams and siding, all parts that be;
We plant the house when we plant the tree.

What do we plant when we plant the tree?
A thousand things that we daily see;
We plant the spire that out-towers the crag,
We plant the staff for our country's flag,
We plant the shade, from the hot sun free;
We plant all these when we plant the tree.

Henry Abbey

All Things Bright and Beautiful

All things bright and beautiful,
　　All creatures great and small,
All things wise and wonderful,
　　The Lord God made them all.

Each little flower that opens,
　　Each little bird that sings,
He made their glowing colours,
　　He made their tiny wings.

The purple-headed mountain,
　　The river running by,
The sunset, and the morning,
　　That brightens up the sky;

The cold wind in the winter,
　　The pleasant summer sun,
The ripe fruits in the garden,
　　He made them every one.

He gave us eyes to see them,
　　And lips that we might tell,
How great is God Almighty,
　　Who has made all things well.

Cecil Frances Alexander

God be in my head

God be in my head,
And in my understanding;

God be in my eyes,
And in my looking;

God be in my mouth,
And in my speaking;

God be in my heart,
And in my thinking;

God be at my end,
And at my departing.

Anonymous
From *The Sarum Missal*

Homage to God

I have seen the waters flow in the river.
I have seen the flowers along the banks of the river.
Passing by, I have gazed upon the countryside
And inhaled the perfume of the orange blossoms.
I have been grateful to God and I have said thank you to him.

Algerian prayer

Index